Put Beginning Readers on the Right Track with
ALL ABOARD READING™

The All Aboard Reading series is especially designed for beginning readers. Written by noted authors and illustrated in full color, these are books that children really want to read—books to excite their imagination, expand their interests, make them laugh, and support their feelings. With fiction and nonfiction stories that are high interest and curriculum-related, All Aboard Reading books offer something for every young reader. And with four different reading levels, the All Aboard Reading series lets you choose which books are most appropriate for your children and their growing abilities.

Picture Readers
Picture Readers have super-simple texts, with many nouns appearing as rebus pictures. At the end of each book are 24 flash cards—on one side is a rebus picture; on the other side is the written-out word.

Station Stop 1
Station Stop 1 books are best for children who have just begun to read. Simple words and big type make these early reading experiences more comfortable. Picture clues help children to figure out the words on the page. Lots of repetition throughout the text helps children to predict the next word or phrase—an essential step in developing word recognition.

Station Stop 2
Station Stop 2 books are written specifically for children who are reading with help. Short sentences make it easier for early readers to understand what they are reading. Simple plots and simple dialogue help children with reading comprehension.

Station Stop 3
Station Stop 3 books are perfect for children who are reading alone. With longer text and harder words, these books appeal to children who have mastered basic reading skills. More complex stories captivate children who are ready for more challenging books.

GROSSET & DUNLAP
Published by the Penguin Group
Penguin Group (USA) Inc., 375 Hudson Street, New York, New York 10014, USA
Penguin Group (Canada), 90 Eglinton Avenue East, Suite 700, Toronto, Ontario M4P 2Y3, Canada
(a division of Pearson Penguin Canada Inc.)
Penguin Books Ltd., 80 Strand, London WC2R 0RL, England
Penguin Group Ireland, 25 St. Stephen's Green, Dublin 2, Ireland (a division of Penguin Books Ltd.)
Penguin Group (Australia), 250 Camberwell Road, Camberwell, Victoria 3124, Australia
(a division of Pearson Australia Group Pty. Ltd.)
Penguin Books India Pvt. Ltd., 11 Community Centre, Panchsheel Park, New Delhi—110 017, India
Penguin Group (NZ), 67 Apollo Drive, Rosedale, North Shore 0632, New Zealand
(a division of Pearson New Zealand Ltd.)
Penguin Books (South Africa) (Pty.) Ltd., 24 Sturdee Avenue,
Rosebank, Johannesburg 2196, South Africa
Penguin Books Ltd., Registered Offices: 80 Strand, London WC2R 0RL, England

ISBN 978-0-448-45572-3   10 9 8 7 6 5 4 3 2 1

nickelodeon™ **The PENGUINS of MADAGASCAR**™

DREAMWORKS®

THE HELMET

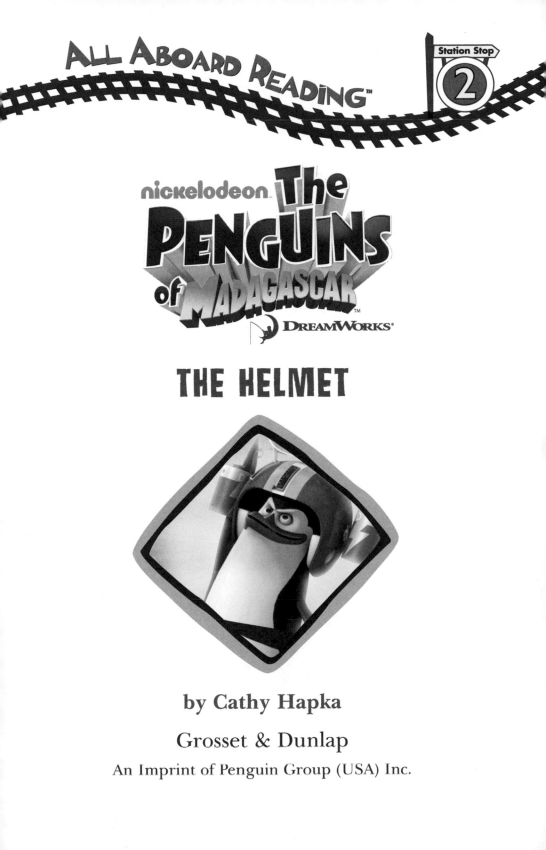

by **Cathy Hapka**

Grosset & Dunlap

An Imprint of Penguin Group (USA) Inc.

It was lunchtime at the New York Zoo.

Rico was making a sandwich.

Well, he was *trying* to make a sandwich.

But it wasn't going well.

First the mayo slid across the table.

Then the fish tried to get away.

Finally the bread ended up on his head!

Rico had no idea what was happening.

Then he heard giggles.

Kowalski, Skipper, and Private stepped out.

"Forgive me, Rico," Kowalski said.

"Just testing my latest invention.

I call it The Helmet!"

Kowalski's new helmet could make
anything he thought really happen!
Soon he had made a perfect sandwich
using only his mind.
He offered to show his friends
what else The Helmet could do.

Meanwhile, in the lemur habitat,

King Julien was doing

a stand-up comedy routine.

Mort and Maurice were watching.

"Maurice's cooking was so bad . . ."

Julien began.

Nobody said anything.

Finally Maurice sighed.

He knew what Julien wanted him to say.

"How bad was it?" he asked.

"It was so bad, I wouldn't eat it!" Julien said.

Mort laughed so hard that he fell over.

Maurice just shook his head.

"But, seriously," Julien went on.

"What is the deal with—" *Oof!*

Suddenly a bunch of fish flew

through the air!

They knocked Julien over.

"Now *that's* funny!" Maurice said.

The Helmet was bringing lots of fish

from all over the city. They were coming

from Kowalski's fish thoughts.

Soon the Penguins had a huge pile.

But they didn't notice Julien

watching them from his throne.

Julien went to visit the Penguins.

"I notice you have a hat that

magically brings you things," he said.

"As king, I have no need for such a hat.

You see, I have Maurice!"

"Kowalski," Skipper said. "Are you thinking

what I'm thinking?"

"Yes," Kowalski said. "But with bigger words."

WHOOSH!

He sent Julien and Maurice

flying back to their own habitat.

The Lemurs landed in a pile.

Now Julien couldn't stop thinking

about the Penguins

and their special helmet.

"I must have that

magic hat!" he cried.

That night, the Penguins slept soundly.

Julien snuck in and tried

to lift The Helmet off Kowalski's head.

It wouldn't budge, so he tried harder.

Finally he yanked The Helmet free

and made his escape.

Kowalski finally woke up.

Something felt different.

"The Helmet!" he cried.

The other penguins woke up, too.

Julien used The Helmet

to bring the Penguins to him.

"Oh, hello," he greeted them.

"How are you liking my new crown?"

"Careful!" Kowalski cried.

"You have no idea of the awesome power

you now hold!"

"Of course I do," Julien said.

"That's why I took it!"

Julien started making The Helmet

bring him lots of snacks.

They flew toward him from all directions.

When something didn't come fast enough,

he turned up the dial on The Helmet.

Then Julien sent the Penguins flying away.

Kowalski was worried.

"He turned the controls up to ten," he said.

"That's way too much

for Julien's extremely limited mind.

His thoughts will destroy us all!"

The Penguins tried to steal back The Helmet.

But Julien caught them.

"I am surrounded by low-down,

dirty snakes!" he cried.

Suddenly he was surrounded by snakes!

"Figure of speech," he said. "Go away!"

Kowalski warned Julien to be careful.

"Whatever you think of

will come to you!" he said.

"Your brain can't handle that kind of power!"

Skipper added.

But Julien wouldn't listen.

He kept talking and thinking

and causing more trouble!

He caused a rhino stampede.

He even made a bus

drive through the zoo!

"My old crown was much less dangerous!"
Julien exclaimed at last.

"So why don't you just take this crown off?"
Skipper suggested.

"Carefully!" Kowalski added.

"Don't think of anything,"

Skipper told Julien.

"I won't!" Julien promised.

"My brain will allow no thoughts in!

My brain will be a brick wall!"

Suddenly a brick wall appeared

between him and the Penguins!

"Oopsie!" Julien called

from the other side of the wall.

Rico knew what to do.

He coughed up a hard hat.

The other penguins used him

to ram their way through the wall.

The Penguins saw Julien trying hard

to control the power of The Helmet.

But he wasn't having much luck.

The Helmet was too strong

for his weak, silly brain!

Suddenly Maurice swung toward Julien.

"Your Highness, I am here to help!" he cried.

He tried to grab The Helmet.

But he was knocked out

by a flying object!

"Oh, Maurice!" Julien cried.

"What have I done?"

"He's distracted, men," Skipper said.

"This is our chance."

Rico knew what to do this time, too.

He coughed up a rocket launcher.

KABOOM!

Rico shot The Helmet

right off Julien's head

and halfway across the zoo.

It exploded in a cloud

of sparks and smoke.

The Helmet was no more.

The zoo was saved!

Maurice coughed.

"Maurice! I thought I lost you!" Julien cried.

"No, but you did lose your hair," Maurice said.

Julien gasped. Maurice was right.

"I am as hairless as a chimp's bottom!"

he cried in horror.

"I've got it covered," Maurice said.

He pulled out Julien's old crown

and set it on the king's head.

"Oh, Maurice," Julien exclaimed.

"You always know just what I need!"

"Well done, Rico," Skipper said
as the Penguins walked away.
They had saved the day,
and the zoo was safe again.
At least until Kowalski created
his next brilliant invention . . .